# A SMALL
# MIRACLE

*Peter Collington*

JONATHAN CAPE

London

For dear Mum

First published 1997

1 3 5 7 9 10 8 6 4 2

Peter Collington has asserted his right under
the Copyright, designs and Patents Act 1988 to be
identified as the author of this work

First published in the United Kingdom
in 1997 by Jonathan Cape Limited, Random House,
20 Vauxhall Bridge Road, London SW1V 2SA

A CIP catalogue record for this book is
available from the British Library

ISBN 0 22404 671 3

Printed in Hong Kong

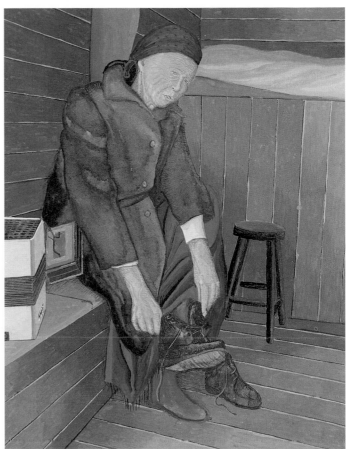

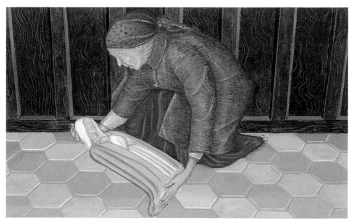